STOLEN KISSES AND BROKEN VOWS:

The Price of Love

Copyright © 2025 by Moses Danso. All rights reserved.

STOLEN KISSES AND BROKEN VOWS

To those who have loved, lost, and dared to love again. May this book be a testament to the enduring power of second chance, and the courage it takes to reclaim a heart once lost.

TABLE OF CONTENTS

Foreword..5

Part 1: The Proposal
Chapter 1: Thirty-Seven Minutes Late...............................6
Chapter 2: The Queen of My Heart....................................7
Chapter 3: A Question on Bended Knee and The Exhoes of The Past...8

Part 2: The Revelation
Chapter 4: A Promise Broken..10
Chapter 5: The Blood Covenant..12

Part 3: Unraveling The Truth
Chapter 6: A Son's Secret..14
Chapter 7: The Weight of Lies and A Glimmer of Hope.16

Part 4: Rebuilding Trust
Chapter 8: The Coffee Shop Confession............................18
Chapter 9: A Promise of Truth..20
Chapter 10: Emefa's Choice and A Second Chance.........21

Part 5: Destiny's Embrace
Chapter 11: A Ring andA Renewed Vow..........................23
About the Author...26

Foreword

appearance and how the dress complemented her beauty.

CHAPTER 2:

The Queen of My Heart

Before I delve into how her presence electrified the party, let me paint a picture of my empress, Asantewaa, so you can appreciate her more. She stands at an average height of about five feet, three inches, with smooth chocolate skin reminiscent of Tacobel pastries. Her thick black hair frames her face, highlighting her visible dimples and a set of sparkling white teeth that could light up a room. Her smile is the most adorable thing on earth; one could only imagine why anyone would want her to cry instead of making her smile every time. Her figure, with its curves and contours, could easily be mistaken for that of Marilyn Monroe, the iconic British actress of the '80s. Sometimes I wonder how foolish I am to think that this enchantress would ever say yes to someone like me, a mere mortal with nothing exceptional to offer. She's clearly out of my league, but I take solace in the belief that women value inner beauty above all else.

The guests at the party were buzzing with excitement. Some had already indulged in plenty of drinks, while others caught up with old friends, thinking about times gone by. Amidst the chatter, I took the microphone from the DJ and captured everyone's attention. With a nervous heart, I dropped to one knee in front of Asantewaa, my hopeful future wife.

CHAPTER 3:

A Question on Bended Knee and The Echoes of The Past

"Asantewaa, you've brought clarity and purpose to my life. You bring out the best in me, and as I kneel before you with humility and sincerity, I ask you, in the presence of our loved ones gathered here today, will you marry me?"

The room fell silent, as if my words had cast a spell, rendering everyone speechless. Tensions mounted, sweat trickled down my back, and my knees went numb. The moment felt surreal. What was taking her so long?

As I knelt on the floor, waiting for Asantewaa's response, my mind drifted back to the distant past, to the days of our childhood when our bond was pure and innocent.

Asantewaa and I had been inseparable since we were kids. We grew up in the same neighborhood, attending the same school and sharing countless adventures together. Even then, there was something special between us, a connection that went beyond mere friendship. But in those carefree days, we never dared to confess our feelings for each other.

Then came the day Asantewaa left for abroad to pursue her studies. It felt like a piece of my heart went with her as she boarded that plane, leaving me behind with only memories of our time together.

Years passed, and I lost touch with Asantewaa. I often wondered where she was and what she was doing, but try as I might, I couldn't find a way to reach her. It wasn't until fate intervened that our paths crossed again.

I remember the day vividly. I was browsing through an art gallery, lost in the beauty of the paintings, when I heard a familiar voice behind me. I turned around to see Asantewaa standing there, a smile lighting up her face. It was as if no time had passed at all.

We spent hours catching up, reminiscing about our childhood adventures and sharing stories of our lives since we last saw each other. But amidst the laughter and nostalgia, there was a shadow lingering over Asantewaa's happiness—the loss of her parents.

Asantewaa's parents had passed away tragically while she was studying abroad, leaving her feeling lost and alone in the world. It was a pain she carried with her every day, a burden that weighed heavily on her heart.

Asantewaa's silence stretches, each second an eternity. Her eyes, usually sparkling, are clouded with a mix of emotions – surprise, sadness, and something I can't quite decipher. She looks down at my kneeling form, then around at the celebrating guests. A single tear rolls down her cheek. She doesn't say yes. Instead, she whispers, "Kwesi, I... I need to show you something."

She takes my hand and leads me away from the party, the music fading behind us. She takes me to a quiet corner, pulls a worn, folded piece of paper from her purse. It's the letter I wrote her as a child, the one I poured my heart into. As she unfolds it, she points to a specific passage, a part I barely remember writing: "...and even though we're just kids now, I promise I'll always be there for you, no matter what. Even if you break my heart, I'll still love you."

Asantewaa looks at me, her eyes filled with pain. "You promised," she says, her voice trembling. "But you weren't there. When my parents... when they were gone, I needed you. And you weren't there."

This was indeed an emotional fallout of the past and the impact of my absence during a difficult time in Asantewaa's life. Can I regain her trust and prove that I am there for her now? Will she grant me a second chance to prove my love for her? It was in the midst of this confused state that she held my hand with a gentle drag back to the party and requested for the microphone to speak. The audience were in awe and intrigued by the dramatic display that had ensued between us.

PART 2:

The Revelation

Chapter 4:

A Promise Broken

Just as she took the microphone from the DJ, Ato, my best friend stumbled forward, clearly intoxicated. He grabbed the microphone and slurred, "Asantewaa, you can't marry him! He's hiding something! He's not who you think he is!"

The music screeched to a halt. All eyes turned to Ato, then to Kwesi. Asantewaa's smile vanished, replaced by confusion and a flicker of hurt. "What is he talking about, Kwesi?" she asked, her voice tight.

Ato, swaying slightly, pointed a finger at Kwesi. "While you were gone, Asantewaa, while you were building your life abroad, he made a blood covenant with another woman! Emefa! And they have a child! A four-year-old boy! He abandoned them both the moment you came back, the moment he realized you'd inherited your parents' wealth!"

The room erupted in whispers. Asantewaa's face paled, her eyes wide with disbelief. Kwesi felt the blood drain from his own face. He looked at Ato, a mixture of anger and betrayal churning within him. He knew this moment would come, but not like this, not so publicly, so cruelly.

He took a deep breath, trying to regain control. "Asantewaa," he said, his voice surprisingly steady, "Ato… Ato is telling the truth. There's something I need to tell you."

void that only you could fill."

He knew it sounded like an excuse, and he hated himself for it. But it was the truth. Or at least, his version of it.

"And now?" Asantewaa asked, her eyes filled with a mixture of hurt and anger. "Now that I'm back, now that I have… resources… you've decided to come clean? Is that it, Kwesi?"

Kwesi's heart sank. He knew how it must look. He had to make her understand that his feelings for her were real, that they had nothing to do with her inheritance.

"No, Asantewaa," he pleaded. "It's not like that. I swear to you, I never knew about your inheritance. When I saw you again, it was like… like coming home. It was like no time had passed at all. I would have proposed to you if you were still… if you were still the girl I grew up with, the girl who had nothing but her dreams."

He reached for her hand again, and this time, she didn't pull away. Her touch was cold, but it gave him a sliver of hope.

"Tell me everything, Kwesi," she said, her voice barely above a whisper. "Tell me the truth. All of it."

Kwesi knew he had a long way to go to earn her forgiveness. But he was willing to do whatever it took. He had to. He had to try. Because Asantewaa was the only woman he had ever truly loved. And he was determined to win her heart, no matter the cost.

As Kwesi began to speak, his voice faltering under the weight of the truth, the garden around them seemed to close in. The distant sounds of the party, the chatter, the music, felt like they were miles away, as if the world had shrunk to this moment—just the two of them and the fractured trust between them.

"I—" Kwesi paused, gathering his thoughts, each word coming with a sharp pang of regret. "After you left, Asantewaa, I was a different person. I didn't know how to cope with the loneliness. When I met Emefa, it felt like… like a chance to escape the emptiness. But that's not an excuse," he added quickly, seeing the skepticism in her eyes. "I was foolish. The bond we shared back then, the memories—none of that changed. But… I made mistakes, and I hurt you, and for that, I can never forgive myself."

Asantewaa's gaze softened for a moment, but her expression remained guarded. "You don't get it, Kwesi," she whispered, almost to herself. "It's not just about the past… it's about everything you've hidden from me, everything you've kept in the shadows. How can I trust you now? How can I believe that this—us—has been real when there's so much you've kept from me?"

Kwesi's heart raced as he watched her pull back emotionally, the distance between them growing with each passing second. He had known this moment might come, but the reality of it was crushing.

"I've spent so long trying to convince myself that I was justified in what I did," he continued, his voice now trembling with emotion, "but there's no justification. I know that. And I know that I've already lost your trust. What I did with Emefa… it wasn't just a mistake—it was a betrayal of you, of everything we had."

Asantewaa remained silent, her eyes cast downward, her fingers clutching the fabric of her dress. The stillness between them was deafening.

And then, just when Kwesi thought he might lose her forever, the air shifted.

PART 3:

Unraveling the Truth

Chapter 6:

A Son's Secret

A sharp, muffled sound came from behind them. The bushes rustled, followed by the faint crunch of gravel underfoot. Kwesi turned instinctively, his pulse quickening.

Out of the corner of his eye, he saw a figure—a shadow moving toward them from the garden gate. It was Emefa.

"Kwesi, I need to talk to you," Emefa's voice cut through the tension like a knife. She stood there, her face pale and determined, but there was something else in her eyes—something desperate.

Asantewaa's head snapped up at the sound of Emefa's voice, her eyes widening in disbelief. "What is she doing here, Kwesi?" Asantewaa's voice was sharp now, her previous sadness replaced by anger.

Kwesi's mind was spinning. He didn't want Asantewaa to see Emefa—especially not now, when everything was on the line. But there was no turning back now. Emefa had come, and her presence was a storm that could either destroy everything or perhaps—just perhaps—be the catalyst for the truth to be fully revealed.

"Emefa, why now?" Kwesi asked, his voice strained, trying to remain calm as the situation spiraled out of control.

Emefa took a step forward, her eyes locked onto Asantewaa, who stood frozen in place, watching her every move. "I need to tell you something, Asantewaa," she said, her voice shaking with emotion.

"Something about Kofi... something Kwesi hasn't told you."

Asantewaa's eyes narrowed. "What could you possibly have to say to me?" she demanded.

Emefa hesitated for a moment, then stepped closer to Kwesi, her eyes full of guilt. "Kofi isn't just Kwesi's son," she said, her words dropping like bombs. "He's yours too. You have a connection to him, Asantewaa. And I think it's time you knew the whole truth."

Kwesi's world seemed to collapse around him as Emefa's words hung in the air. Asantewaa staggered back, her hand flying to her mouth in shock. "What do you mean?" she gasped, her voice barely a whisper.

CHAPTER 7:

The Weight of Lies and A Glimmer of Hope

Emefa glanced at Kwesi, then turned to face Asantewaa, her expression a mix of regret and resolve. "When we made that blood covenant, it wasn't just about promises between Kwesi and me. There was something else... something unspoken. Kofi wasn't just born out of a relationship. He was... part of a larger plan—something much bigger than either of us realized."

Kwesi stood there, feeling the floor drop out from beneath him. He had tried so hard to keep his past buried, to build something new with Asantewaa, but now, everything was unraveling before his eyes.

"How could you keep this from me?" Asantewaa cried, her voice cracking as she took a step back, her face pale. "How could you not tell me about my own son?"

Kwesi's heart broke as he tried to explain, but nothing he said seemed to be enough. The weight of the truth was too heavy to bear. And now, it seemed like he had lost not only Asantewaa's trust but possibly her love too.

But as Asantewaa turned to leave, her footsteps echoing in the silence of the garden, Kwesi felt an overwhelming sense of desperation. He wasn't ready to lose her—not like this, not without fighting for her.

"Please, Asantewaa," he begged, stepping forward and grabbing her arm gently. "Let me explain. Please. I know I've hurt you, but I need you to know the whole story. You deserve to know everything."

Asantewaa's eyes flickered with a mix of anger, confusion, and pain. "I don't know if I can forgive you for this, Kwesi," she whispered. "But I need time. Time to think. Time to understand why everything has been so complicated."

With that, she pulled away from him, walking toward the gate, leaving him standing there in the dim light of the garden, uncertain of what the future would hold.

And as the night wore on, Kwesi realized that he would have to fight harder than ever before to win back the woman he loved—and to uncover the full truth about the ties that bound them together, even in the darkest of times.

The following days were a blur for Kwesi. He could barely focus at work, his thoughts constantly drifting to Asantewaa. He had never felt more alone, more detached from the world around him, than he did in those painful, restless nights. His phone remained silent—no texts, no calls from Asantewaa. Every time he thought of reaching out, the weight of the truth between them stopped him. How could he possibly explain everything?

He knew he had to act quickly before Asantewaa completely shut him out. He needed to show her that he wasn't the same man who had made mistakes in the past. He had to prove that he was worthy of her trust again.

Kwesi found himself at the local coffee shop where he and Asantewaa had once spent hours talking, laughing, and dreaming about the future. He sat at their usual table, his hands wrapped around a cup of lukewarm coffee, waiting for any sign of her.

His mind was a storm. The memory of Emefa's revelation weighed heavily on him. He still couldn't fully comprehend what Emefa had meant about Kofi being connected to Asantewaa. But there was one thing he was sure of—if he could get Asantewaa to understand the truth, maybe she would give him a chance to make things right.

The door to the coffee shop chimed as someone walked in. Kwesi's heart skipped a beat as he turned, hoping against hope that it was Asantewaa. But when he saw her standing in the doorway, her eyes still filled with the same hurt and confusion, his breath caught in his throat.

She hesitated for a moment, then walked toward him. She didn't sit down immediately. Instead, she stood in front of him, her arms crossed, her gaze piercing.

PART 4:

Rebuilding Trust

Chapter 8:

The Coffee Shop Confession

"I need to know everything, Kwesi," she said, her voice steady but full of underlying emotion. "I need you to tell me the truth—everything about Emefa, about Kofi, and about what this blood covenant really means. I need to know if this is something I can trust you with."

Kwesi nodded, his throat tight. This was it. The moment he'd been dreading and hoping for. He knew that if he didn't tell her everything now, he might lose her forever.

"Asantewaa," he began, his voice shaky but firm, "I'm sorry for everything. For the lies, the secrets, the way I tried to bury my past. I didn't want to hurt you. I didn't want you to see me for who I was, someone who made mistakes, someone who failed you when you needed me the most."

Asantewaa's eyes softened slightly, but she didn't interrupt him. He continued, "When you left, I didn't know how to handle the loneliness. I felt like I was losing you all over again. That's when I met Emefa. It was a time in my life when I wasn't the man I am now. I was lost. Emefa and I... we made a blood covenant because we were both broken in different ways. It was supposed to be a way for us to bind ourselves together, to promise that no matter what happened, we would stay committed to each other."

"But that was a lie," he continued, his voice breaking. "The moment you came back into my life, I realized how foolish I had been. I realized that I never stopped loving you, that no one could ever fill the void you left in me. I thought Emefa was my way of escaping the pain, but all it did was create a bigger mess."

Asantewaa remained silent, her eyes searching his face for any sign of dishonesty. Kwesi took a deep breath, trying to find the courage to continue.

"And about Kofi," he said, his voice low, "Emefa and I... we had a son. But the truth is, when you left, I thought we'd never see each other again. I convinced myself that I was doing the right thing by moving on, but when you came back, everything changed. I realized that the life I thought I could have with Emefa was a lie. Kofi is my son, but I never wanted to keep him from you or anyone else."

He paused, wiping his brow. "The connection Emefa was talking about... it's because, in that moment of desperation, I made a promise. A promise that had nothing to do with your inheritance or anything material. I made a promise to be there for Emefa, to help her raise Kofi. But when you came back, I knew that I couldn't live in both worlds. I had to choose. And I chose you, Asantewaa."

Tears welled up in his eyes as he looked at her, hoping she could see the sincerity in his heart. "I know I've hurt you. I know I've made mistakes that have shattered your trust in me. But please, Asantewaa, give me a chance to prove that I can be the man you deserve. I know it's not going to be easy. I know it's going to take time. But I'm willing to fight for you. For us."

Asantewaa looked at him for a long time, her face unreadable. Kwesi's heart pounded in his chest, each second feeling like an eternity. He could feel the weight of his confession hanging in the air between them, and he feared that his words might not be enough.

CHAPTER 9:

A Promise of Truth

Finally, she spoke.

"I don't know if I can trust you again, Kwesi," she said softly. "You've lied to me, hidden things from me. And I don't know if I can ever forget that."

Kwesi's stomach dropped, but he refused to back down. "I don't expect you to forgive me right away. But I'll be here, every step of the way, showing you that I'm not the man I was before. I love you, Asantewaa. I always have, and I always will."

She looked at him for a long moment, her expression unreadable. Then, just when he thought he might have lost her forever, she reached out and placed a hand on his.

"I don't know if I can trust you again," she whispered, "but I'm willing to try. Just... promise me one thing."

Kwesi's heart skipped a beat. "Anything," he said, his voice hoarse with emotion.

"Promise me that no matter what happens," she said, her voice steady, "you'll never hide anything from me again. That we will face everything together. That the truth will always be out in the open."

Kwesi nodded, tears streaming down his face. "I promise," he said, his voice thick with emotion. "I will never hide anything from you again."

And in that moment, Asantewaa squeezed his hand, a small but significant gesture. It wasn't forgiveness. Not yet. But it was a beginning—a new chapter in their journey, one where trust could be rebuilt, and where love could heal the wounds of the past.

As they sat together in silence, Kwesi realized that the cost of love was high. But if he was willing to pay it, maybe—just maybe—he could find his way back to her heart.

As time passed, Kwesi and Asantewaa began to rebuild what had been lost. It wasn't easy. There were moments of doubt, times when the shadow of the past loomed over their growing relationship, but they worked through them together. The love they shared was undeniable, and the bond that had always existed between them slowly started to heal the wounds of betrayal and hurt.

But there was still one more obstacle to overcome.

CHAPTER 10:

Emefa's Choice and a Second Chance

Emefa had been quiet for a while, retreating into herself as she processed the chaos that had unfolded. Kwesi had made it clear to her that, while he would always care for their son, his heart belonged to Asantewaa. And while it had been difficult, Emefa had come to accept it. She had once been a part of Kwesi's life, but now, she knew that his future was with Asantewaa.

One afternoon, Kwesi received a call from Emefa. He braced himself for the conversation, unsure of what to expect.

"Kwesi," Emefa's voice came through the line, steady but tinged with emotion. "I've been thinking a lot. And I realized something. I can't hold onto you forever. You and Asantewaa... it's clear that you belong together. You've always been connected, and I can see that your love for each other is real."

Kwesi felt a mix of relief and sadness. He'd always known that it wouldn't be easy for Emefa to let go, especially with Kofi involved, but hearing her words now felt like the final step in the journey of letting go of his past mistakes.

"Kwesi," Emefa's voice was tight, laced with a sadness I hadn't heard before. "I've been doing a lot of thinking. About Kofi. About us. About you and Asantewaa." She paused, taking a shaky breath. "I see the way you look at her, Kwesi. It's... it's not something you can fake. And Kofi... he deserves to have parents who are truly together, truly in love. I can't give him that. Not the way Asantewaa can. And honestly," she admitted, her voice dropping to a whisper, "I'm tired of pretending. Pretending that what we had was real, pretending that I could ever truly have you. I love Kofi. I'll always love him. And that's why I have to do this. For him. For Asantewaa. And maybe… just maybe… for myself."

"Thank you, Emefa," Kwesi said softly, his heart full of gratitude. "I promise you; Kofi will always be a part of my life. I'll never turn my back on him. And I'll make sure he grows up knowing the truth—that he was loved by both his parents, even if our paths were different."

Emefa paused before speaking again. "I hope you and Asantewaa find the happiness you deserve. I truly do."

With that, their conversation ended. The weight of the past seemed to lift from Kwesi's shoulders, and for the first time in years, he felt like he was truly moving forward. Asantewaa was by his side, and together, they had weathered the storm.

One evening, as they sat on the porch, Kwesi turned to Asantewaa, who was looking at him with a playful glint in her eyes.

"You know," she said, her voice teasing, "you never did give me that ring you promised me."

Kwesi's heart skipped a beat. "You still want it?" he asked, surprised but hopeful.

Asantewaa shrugged, a smile tugging at her lips. "Well, you made quite the dramatic proposal back at that party, and I think I deserve to at least have the ring, don't you think?"

PART 5:

Destiny's Embrace

Chapter 11:

A Ring and a Renewed Vow

Kwesi chuckled, his nerves returning as he reached into his pocket. He pulled out the small velvet box and opened it to reveal the ring that had once been meant for a future uncertain. Now, it symbolized a love that had weathered storms and survived the trials of life.

"Asantewaa," he said, his voice steady but filled with emotion, "I know I've made mistakes, but I will never make the mistake of letting you go. I love you with all my heart, and I will spend the rest of my life proving it to you."

Asantewaa's eyes sparkled with laughter, but she held up a hand. "Wait, wait," she said, her voice teasing but warm. "You forgot something."

Kwesi blinked, confused. "What did I forget?"

She grinned, her eyes full of mischief. "You forgot to kneel. Again."

Kwesi's heart swelled with love and relief as he realized what she was asking. He grinned, his hands shaking slightly as he lowered himself to one knee in front of her.

"Asantewaa," he said again, the words pouring out of him as if they had been waiting for this moment, "Will you marry me?"

Tears filled Asantewaa's eyes as she looked down at him, her heart full of joy. "Yes," she whispered, her voice trembling. "Yes, Kwesi, I will."

Kwesi slid the ring onto her finger, and they both stood, holding each other tightly. The future was no longer uncertain. They had made it through the hardest parts, and now, all that mattered was their love.

And as they stood there, the weight of the past finally lifting from their shoulders, Kwesi knew one thing for sure: no matter what happened in the future, their love was destined to survive, to thrive, and to carry them through the rest of their lives.

Together.

THE END

ABOUT THE AUTHOR

Moses Danso is the author of "Stolen Kisses and Broken Vows." Born in Tema, Ghana, on November 26, 1989, Moses finds inspiration in the resilience of the human spirit and the enduring power of love. He believes in the transformative potential of storytelling and hopes his words resonate with readers long after they turn the final page. By day, Moses works as an Anaesthetist, carefully attending to the well-being of others, a dedication that also informs his writing.

When not writing, Moses enjoys exploring nature's beauty through long walks, finding serenity in the water while swimming, and dedicating his time to charitable causes that make a difference.

Made in the USA
Columbia, SC
19 February 2025